THE MAGIC BOOTS

Story by SCOTT EMERSON and HOWARD POST

Illustrated by HOWARD POST

GIBBS·SMITH PUBLISHER

SALT LAKE CITY

02 01 00 99 5 4 3 2 1

Published by
Gibbs Smith, Publisher
P.O. Box 667
Layton, Utah 84041

Book design by Traci O'Very Covey
Printed in Hong Kong

Library of Congress Cataloging-in-Publication Data

Emerson, Scott, 1959-

The magic boots / story by Scott Emerson and Howard Post;
illustrated by Howard Post.

p. cm

Summary: William has a pair of magic cowboy boots that take him
wherever he wants to go, but when he outgrows them, he makes a
surprising discovery.

ISBN 0-87905-603-7
ISBN 0-87905-874-9 (pbk.)

[1. Boots—Fiction. 2. Imagination—Fiction.] I. Post, Howard,
1948- ill. II. Title.
PZ7.E5857Mag 1994   94-4036
[E]—dc20   CIP
                                                       AC

DEDICATED

to the magic of childhood

Every morning when
William Wilkins got out of bed, he
brushed his teeth, patted his dog,
Bob, and put on his cowboy boots.

They weren't just ordinary boots.
For one thing, they were bright
red. They were soft, too, as soft
as Bob's ears.

But the most unordinary thing
about William's cowboy boots
was this: they were magic.

They weren't
magic in the usual way.
They didn't glow or throw
off sparks or walk around
by themselves. A miniature
genie didn't live inside
them. But when William
put them on, he could go
anywhere he wanted.

All he had to do
was think of a place,
anyplace, and in the blink
of an eye he was there.

Just like that.

Once, he went canoeing down the Amazon River.

One time,
he spent the day
with Buffalo Bill's
Wild West Show.

And since he had always wanted to be a cowboy, at least once a week he took a herd of longhorns up the Chisholm Trail.

With the help of
the magic boots, William
travelled the world . . .
and he soon discovered that
all he had to do was hold
real tight, and Bob could
travel right along with him.

He made new friends,

and he learned to see things
from a different point of view.

But then, one day, it happened.
The most horrible, dreadful, ghastly, rotten,
worst thing William could imagine:
his feet would not fit inside the boots.

He took his socks off and sprinkled baby
powder on his feet. It didn't help.

He soaked his feet in ice water, hoping they
would shrink. They didn't.

F inally, he faced the awful truth. His feet were just too big. He had outgrown the magic boots. All day long, he moped around, feeling sorry for himself, wishing he didn't have to grow up.

His mother tried everything to make him feel better. She even took him to get a new pair of high-tops.

It didn't help.

William couldn't get used to the idea that he would never again explore the Amazon, walk on the moon, or visit the Wild West.

That night, he cried himself to sleep, thinking about all the places he would never see again.

nd suddenly,

he was back on the Chisholm Trail . . .

saving the Princess from the Black Knight . . .

and hang gliding over the Grand Canyon.

ut when he looked
down, expecting to see the
magic boots, all he saw were his
own bare feet.

And at that moment, he realized it
wasn't the boots that were magic.

It was him.

In the morning,
he bounded out of bed,
brushed his teeth until
they sparkled, gave Bob
a big hug, and put on
his new high-tops.

Then, as William stepped
out the back door,
he thought of a place
far away . . .

and in the blink of
an eye, he was there.